Mrs O'Leary has a GREAT I
league! To keep all the tea-
place out of trouble. And g
which might come in handy in view of
impending Council elections.

Riverside to a man – or a U-14 – rise to the challenge. Which team will bring home the Brenda O'Leary Perpetual Cup?

But, of course, football is not the only thing their minds. Chippy has his gran to worry . Jimmy has to sort out his da, write a and dream about the beautiful Heather dden. Mad Victor has his own ideas; ially where Mrs O'Leary is concerned …

R REGAN, born in north Roscommon, ives in Bray, where he runs a small fuel seed business. He writes about soccer from ersonal experience; he once managed a hoolboy team, and as 'Chick' Regan asterminded the Avon Glens and Brighton ic. Today he is a spectator, following the unes of Liverpool and Glasgow Celtic.

He has written three soccer books: *Urban oes, Teen Glory* and *Young Champions,* which e been very successful here and have also en translated into several European nguages. He has also written two fantasy ks: *Touchstone* and *Revenge of the Wizards.*

BRIGID O'BRIEN
BORN 1894
DIED 1976
R.I.P.

Peter Regan

RIVERSIDE

The Street-League

Illustrated by Terry Myler

THE CHILDREN'S PRESS

For
Ruth Bourke
Born 3 December 1995

First published 1996 by
The Children's Press
45 Palmerston Road, Dublin 6

4 6 5

ISBN 0 947962 46 8

Typeset by Computertype Limited
Printed by Colour Books Limited

Contents

Us against Fassaroe!
sure, it'd be just brill!
Us against Wolfe Tone!

1 Mrs O'Leary's Idea

My name is Jimmy Quinn. My da is also named Jimmy. My granda too, only he is dead. He died in the house. His eyes were big and starey, and they put fifty-pence pieces on them so as people coming into the room couldn't see him stare. I though that was stupid, because dead people can't see, unless they're ghosts, and Granda was no ghost.

'Da, why are we all called "Jimmy"?'

'Cause we're all named after Granda, an' he came from Belfast. An' every second fella in Belfast is called Jimmy, that's why.'

'What brought him down here?'

We were from Dublin. Every one of us were Dubs, all except Granda.

His last words weren't words as such. More of a song: *It's a long way to Tipperary*. He sang it in a Belfast accent. It was a real tragedy. My da was heartbroken.

I remember my granda real well. He was a

refugee from the Troubles. Don't ask me which Troubles. He went around on a nobbly stick. He'd often give me a whack of it. He was a hearty old soul. He fought in the War.

He had a hatred of small people and that's why I got hit so much. I was only beginning to grow. He thought I was a Jap; not that I looked like one, but he thought I did.

Although all my family were born Dubs we moved to a council estate in Bray when I was younger. The snobs call Palermo, the council estate we live on, 'Hungry Hill'. It's not that bad really. But the snobs like to think it is. They like to think we're all starving. But nothing could be further from the truth. It's just plain lies. But we're stuck with the name. Stuck with 'Hungry Hill'.

I'm an only son, though I have two sisters, Fiona and Kathleen My sisters are years older than me. I'm only fourteen. I'm dying for them to run away. But so far nothing has happened. They go out every Friday and Saturday night. But they always come back, worse luck.

I'll be mentioning my family a lot. But I'm

not really into families, I'm more into football, and that's what I'm going to talk about most – not big-time football, but the 'you and me' type of football.

You see, I'm a football nutter.

I always wanted to be a footballer. All the kids around our way want to be footballers. We all dream of playing for Man United, Liverpool and the likes. That's why, in the schoolyard, we all have notions we're playing for United, and all that.

Sometimes I think I'm Ryan Giggs. I'm good with the left foot, not always, but sometimes things connect and it all comes good for me. Butcher Hayes thinks he's Eric Cantona. He'd break you in half with Kung-Fu kicks. We're all in Second Year and the only subject he takes seriously is French. Yeah, he's that keen on Eric the Red.

Our local soccer club is Riverside Boys. I play for the U-14s. So do some of the other lads. The rest just mess; they're not good enough to play for a real team. But that's the best about soccer – you can have 'mess teams'.

That way everybody gets a game.

Talking about 'mess teams', a real dream happened at the start of the summer, just after the season with Riverside Boys ended. Mrs O'Leary, who lives up the road from our estate, got a street-league going.

'Wha's a street-league?' one of the nippers asked me.

'It's a league made up of different streets, or estates. You have a meetin' and draw up a list of the streets, or areas, the players have to be from, and the age they've to be.'

'Sayin' if next to no kids live on a road, wha' then?'

'Well, maybe the whole estate could be taken in instead. That's why there has to be a meetin' to draw up rules and the likes. Then there has to be someone to run the whole thing.'

'That's what Mrs O'Leary is then?'

Mrs O'Leary a runner-of-things? More of a meddler really. She always carries a handbag, and kicks up murder because there's no place for kids to play. She's kind of fat, and her hair

is dyed carrot red. Her face is wrinkly, and she wears clothes something like people used to wear sixty years ago.

My da said she is a kind of old-age Bernadette Devlin, whoever she was, fighting for people's rights. She is always beating a path to the Council offices, highlighting the lack of playgrounds and the danger of getting run over by cars.

She's dead nuts on cars. I've seen her batter a few with her handbag. She's real nifty with her handbag. She can fight her corner all right

– once her handbag is at the ready.

For Mrs O'Leary, Monday, Tuesday, Wednesday and Thursday are all good days to go to the Council offices to lodge a complaint.

Friday is out, as Friday is the start of the weekend cabaret acts. Mrs O'Leary loves going to cabaret, and there's this fellow who does Dickie Rock on a Friday night, and Mrs O'Leary's mad keen on Dickie Rock so Friday is out for the Council offices as she wants to be in a good humour for the cabaret.

Anyway, Mrs O'Leary held a meeting and drew up rules for the estates to play against one another in the street-league. The competition was to be U-14 which just suited me and my pals. George Glynn, my manager at Riverside Boys, wasn't too pleased though, as he thought a new club might spring up out of the street-league in opposition to Riverside. He was dead worried about that, him and his sidekick, Harry Hennessy, but he needn't have worried. The street-league was only for a laugh; only the managers took it serious. They nearly cracked up over it. Them and Mrs O'Leary.

Liam Molloy, who sells coal around Bray, told us all about the street-league. Usually, especially in the winter, his ears are so full of coal dust he can't hear anything. You have to shout at him most of the time.

'Wolfe Tone, Fassaroe, Palermo, Charnwood, Seacrest, Oldcourt, Ballywaltrim, Woodbrook Lawn, Ardmore Park and Woodbrook Glen are the teams,' he shouted.

Shouted? For some reason, people who can't hear always shout. 'Mrs O'Leary from Fassaroe is in charge of it all. I told her I'd run the Palermo team. I suppose I might as well do me bit. I couldn't very well refuse, could I?'

'You sure you'll be able to manage the team, Liam?'

'Wha' d'ye mean?'

'Well, you've never run a team before. You mightn't be able for the job.'

'Course I'll be able. I've seen it all on the telly. I've played too. I know a bit.'

We all knew he'd played football, kick-about football. That's what worried us. He'd be a dead loss as a manager. But we weren't too worried. We'd be well able to do the job ourselves, training and all. We hadn't put in four years with Riverside and learned nothing. We knew the game inside out, or so we thought.

'When's the league due to start, Liam?'

'Middle of June, Jimmy. When your football season's over. I can't wait to get started.'

Neither could we. We fancied our chances. We'd stuff all the other estates. June? We could hardly wait to get at them.

Us against Fassaroe!

Us against Wolfe Tone!

Sure, it'd be just brill!

2 Chippy's Gran

One of my best pals, 'Chippy' O'Brien, who lives in Fassaroe, just across from Palermo, told me a secret a few months ago. He told me to tell no one, meaning I'd tell the whole of Bray – if they'd believe me, that is.

He told me on the way home from football training one night. What he said made me so scared I kept the bedroom light on all night.

Chippy told me his gran was a banshee, and that she went around haunting people.

'I'll bring you down to see her some night,' he said.

'Where?'

'She hangs out in the graveyard, just down from your estate.'

There is a graveyard in our estate. It's called St Peter's. It's only about a hundred yards from where I live. I can see it, no bother, from the top windows of the house.

Chippy told me all about his granny, the

banshee. Brigid is her name.

'You see,' he told me, 'me and my gran have a chat now and again. I can see ghosts and banshees and talk to them without anybody else knowing about it. I usually meet her at night, sitting on the graveyard wall on the way down to the chipper. She asks me to go to the Coach and Horses to buy her a bottle of stout. It's not easy to get the bottle of stout, me bein' underage. But I get it. My gran hasn't much time for football though.'

'I don't believe a word of it, especially her drinkin' stout. Banshees don't drink stout.'

'Well, my gran does. She drinks Guinness all the time. Give's a pound and I'll bring you to see her sometime.'

'Why should I hand over a pound?'

'It's a pound to see her.'

'Give off!'

'A pound's cheap. I'm doin' it cheap for you, cause you're me friend.'

'If I am, you should do it for nothin'.'

'No, I need the money. I have to buy her Guinness, don't I? Guinness costs money.'

I wasn't going to give Chippy a pound to see any banshee. I'd go down some night on my own and see her for nothing, that's as soon as I plucked up the courage. It took a while, but I finally made it. I couldn't see her sitting on the wall like Chippy said she would be.

I called out her name, 'Brigid! Brigid!'

There wasn't a stir.

I mentioned a few things Chippy told me about her in the hope she'd come out over the graveyard wall and I'd get a good look at her. Personal things like the duck eggs she used to sell to visitors on Bray seafront when she was a young girl.

While I was calling for Brigid to come over the wall, Porky Davis, a neighbour of ours, was passing by.

'Talking to yerself again, Jimmy?' he said.

'Naw, there's a kitten stuck over the wall. I'm tryin' to get it out.'

'You wouldn't want to be talkin' like that, you'll end up in the nuthouse.'

The nuthouse was a sore point with me. I'd been told not to be talking to myself loads of times. Anyway, Porky Davis is pure scruffy. If you wanted to hide money from him the best place to put it would be under a bar of soap.

Porky stood there watching me. He wouldn't shove off.

So as to make it look like I was looking for a kitten I had to get over the wall.

'Want any help?'

'No.'

I peeped back over the wall. He was going off down the road. I was rid of him.

Now that I was in the graveyard I didn't feel so brave. I kept quiet. I wasn't in any humour to meet a banshee. Next thing, I kind of lost my balance. I put my hand on a headstone to steady myself. I looked down. Between the moonlight and the light from the pole outside on the road I read what was written on the headstone:

BRIGID O'BRIEN
Born 1894
Died 1976
R.I.P.

Straight away I wondered if the headstone belonged to Chippy's granny.

Just then something began to howl. It was the banshee!

I took off like a light, leapt over the graveyard wall and ran home. I didn't stop until I got up the stairs and into the bedroom. I drew the curtains and bolted the door. I didn't budge until it was time to get up for school the next day.

Just then I felt Chippy's banshee was for real. There was a fair chance he was telling the truth.

3 Flying Freddy

Apart from football, I've always fancied writing a book. Ever since I was knee-high, I felt this urge come over me. I'd write on anything, copybooks, library books, bus tickets, the wallpaper, anything that didn't move.

'I'm goin' to write a book,' I told my da.

'Write a book! You can hardly write your name.'

The Da, he doesn't exactly give one confidence. He's always giving out. Always saying, 'You're useless.' Well, if I was like him I'd be useless, but I'm not. I'm my own man. I'm only fourteen, but I'm man enough to out-think most of the old lads that live around here. Well, you wouldn't see any of them being able to go head over heels, stand on their heads and smoke a fag at the same time, or down a pint of lemonade in between drags.

I can do all that. I can do almost anything. I was even going to run away and join the circus, only I knew the Da would find me. He'd nag me for the rest of my life over it. He's like that – he's a shadow that won't go away. When I die he'll be there in the coffin beside me.

'Oh, you're here,' I'll say. Then he'll answer, 'Course I'm here. I'm God you know.'

It'll be just my luck if Da is God – the Devil more likely. He's not all bad. But worse than half bad – almost two-thirds bad.

Ma's all right though. When she heard I was going to write a book she bought a Parker pen, seven copybooks, a dictionary and a cushion for the chair I was going to sit on.

'Wha's a dict…shun…ary, Ma?'

'It'll help your command of English. All great writers have a command of English.'

'I'm not thick, Ma. I mean I know what words mean.'

'It'll help your spelling then.'

Spellings were a weak point. I was never much good at spellings. But that wasn't going to put me off, I wanted so badly to write a book. Then the what's-its-name would be a crutch that would help me overcome my problem.

I thought I'd get a poke at Da.

'Da, does bad spelling run in families?'

'No, it's a disease you pick up at school.'

Da always lies. He's a good liar because he believes every word he says.

'Write a book!' he shouted. 'You have to know about life before you're able to write a book.' I knew what he was really about. He was trying to give me the heave-ho before I'd even started.

Know about life! The phrase struck a chord. Once I heard a baldy fellow on the telly saying, 'Write what you know about.' In fact, people are always saying, 'Write what you know about,' on the telly.

So I decided I'd write a football story. I'd write about my football team, Riverside Boys. I'd write about my manager, Mr Glynn, and Harry Hennessy, the greatest referee that ever lived. Maybe I'd even write about Mrs O'Leary and the street-league.

The street-league went fairly okay. Well, as okay as could be expected, considering Mrs O'Leary kept interfering. She didn't like the goal-posts, said they were too big, and all because Fassaroe, the estate she was from, had a small goal-keeper. It was easy to chip the ball over his head, he hadn't a chance.

'You'll have to make the goal-posts smaller.'

'Why?'

'Freddy Fox can't reach the ball.'

'It's the same for everybody, Mrs O'Leary.'

'Not for Freddy Fox.'

Fassaroe played all their home matches on a small green at the back of the estate. So Mrs O'Leary had the rules twisted so Fassaroe could use small goal-posts and put Freddy Fox on a parity (her word) with the other goal-keepers.

'Wha's a parity, Missus?' asked some thick.

'Parity – the same, as in equal.'

'It's not our fault he's so small, Mrs O'Leary.'

'Who says he's small?' ranted Mrs O'Leary. 'Look, his father's six-foot-six. He'll be the same some day. Don't be pickin' on him just because he's small.'

'We're not pickin' on him, Mrs O'Leary. It's just the goal-posts look stupid. They're like hockey posts.'

Mrs O'Leary said nothing. Her eyelids squashed shut and she puckered her lips like a goldfish. She wasn't far from losing her temper. All the usual signs were there. We could tell. Just the same way some people can tell the weather. We said nothing, just kept quiet and out of reach, in case we'd get a belt of her handbag.

In all the matches that were played, Fassaroe never lost a home game. Freddy Fox leapt all over the place. One-handed saves, smothered half-shots, they were all the same to Freddy Fox, the four-and-a-half-foot marvel.

If Mrs O'Leary could juggle the rules to suit Freddy, we felt we could do the same with Freddy's name. We thought of a new one for him: 'Freddy Frog, Wonder Runt'.

Of the other teams, Wolfe Tone, Oldcourt and Ardmore were the only real threat, although Charnwood weren't bad. They had

this player, Andrew Healy, who was dead keen on catching birds. Andrew was cute as a fox. We never liked playing against him. He was real sly in front of goal. He'd play dumb on purpose. And once you thought he was no threat he'd come alive and pop the ball into the back of the net.

He was the same with birds. He used to cycle everywhere with a goldfinch in a cage and bits of branches hanging off his bike. He'd go on a tour of the fields on the outskirts of town and prop up the bits of branches and hope the goldfinch would attract other birds to land in the boughs. He'd have this sticky stuff all over the branches. And once the birds landed they stuck to the stuff. He'd grab them quick, rub the sticky stuff off, and pop them into the cage.

One day, the Wildlife caught up with Andrew. They took his cage, sticky stuff and all, and he was brought to Court and cautioned. He got off but was warned never to catch birds again.

Like a true birdman he only played one position on the pitch – on the wing. He wouldn't play anywhere else.

4 The Wolfe Toners

I had plenty of ideas for my book. It was time to get started. I knew I had to get into some kind of routine – get the Parker and paper out and fill in the sheets of white paper with words. That was the least of my worries, or so I thought. I was always good at talking words; it was getting them down on the page was what really mattered. Getting them down in a way that would make sense.

'Writing is like being a general in the Army,' I mouthed, facing the bathroom mirror early one morning. 'And all the words are your soldiers. You order them about. Shout and curse them into shape. You can turn words into Rambos, Clint Eastwood, or St Francis of Assisi if you like. After all you are a writer, a master of words, a maker-up of stories.'

My two sisters nearly cracked-up when they heard that. They were standing outside the bathroom door waiting to come in. They always used the bathroom together. They did everything together, well almost everything.

'You're in there half an hour. Hurry up or we'll tell Da.'

'Tell him. It won't register. He doesn't wake up until it's time to watch Sesame Street.'

'Come on out!'

'I'm not done!'

'All you're doin' is talkin' to yourself.'

'I could be doin' worse. Give a fella a break. Go outside and use the bushes.'

'We don't want that. We want to wash.'

'Stand in the rain. It's good for the skin.'

Sisters! Who would have them? The bathroom was full of their stuff. Bottles and packs and jars. You name it. A bit of tracing paper would have done them fine. Trace it over a map of Africa and put it on their faces. Sisters! They weren't going to be in my book; that was for certain.

I hadn't had a chance to talk to Chippy about my run-in with the banshee in the graveyard. Every time I met him he seemed to be in a hurry. But I finally cornered him.

'I was in the graveyard a few nights ago.'

'You were?'

'I heard a howl. Somethin' like a mad cat, only I thought it was a banshee.'

'Did you get a fright?'

'Course I did.'

'Did you run for your life?'

'No, I didn't.' I wasn't going to tell him I ran all the way home. 'I just had a look around. Saw nothin' and went home.'

'Sure?'

'Course I'm sure.'

'We'll go down tonight. I'll make sure you get a good look at her.'

All of a sudden I wasn't too sure I wanted to see Chippy's granny.

'You're not afraid?'

'No. I don't have to pay a pound, do I?'

'No. I'll let you see her for free.'

That night Chippy brought me to the graveyard. When we got there he started shouting, 'Granny! Granny! Where are you?' But nothing happened. There wasn't a trace of her.

Then Chippy started acting real worried. 'Maybe she's gone off and got lost. Maybe she's gone to a different graveyard by mistake. Somethin' like what old people do when they're in hospital and get into the wrong bed. Maybe she's sufferin' from Alz…Alzheimer's Disease! Granny are you there?'

No, Granny wasn't there. We headed off and went up the town to one of the snooker halls. Chippy knew the man in charge, so we got a game for free. Only it wasn't quite free for me. Chippy won fifty-pence off me.

It was the only fifty-pence I had.

One of the crunch matches for us in the street-league would be away to Wolfe Tone, or so we thought. Wolfe Tone was at the opposite end of the town to us.

'Wolfe Toners' we called them.

Them.

Us.

It was always them and us.

Just up from our football pitch there's a bridge that connects to the Main Street and the rest of the town. Lads from our side of the bridge hate lads from the other side, and likewise. There's a tradition that the best footballers come from our side of the bridge. Wolfe Toners don't agree. They always think *they* are the best.

Maybe there's another reason for this. Maybe it's because our end of the town is older than Wolfe Tone and the other estates. What I'm trying to say is that soccer took its roots from our end of the town, especially around the streets beside our football pitch. Wolfe Tone only got going years after us. They used to play on the street, using lamp-posts as goal-posts, the older ones keeping the game going, especially during the summer, until two o'clock in the morning. The squad-car was a regular caller at late-night games.

'It's the cops.'

'To hell with them.'

'They'll take names.'

'So what? There's plenty of names. Don' forget, Jesus had twelve apostles. We'll give their names.'

Wolfe Toners weren't for scarpering, they always stood their ground. And no matter how many times the squad-car came around the Wolfe Toners talked their way out of trouble by giving wrong names. In the end the Gardai got fed up and left them to themselves.

After some years, Wolfe Tone's nearest neighbour, a rich lord, gave them a field to play on. The lord owned Bray Head and all the land for miles around. His ancestors were Normans. They had lived in Bray before Bray was ever a town, a village, a house. They took over the whole place.

Anybody in Bray who speaks with a posh accent is of Norman descent, so my da told me. Especially if they have a posh accent *and* are into riding horses. Makes sense, doesn't it?

After a few years of playing football in the lord's field the Wolfe Toners became class footballers. Then the lord gave them a beautiful pitch in the Vevay where they now play. He didn't give them the lovely pavilion, though. They built that themselves.

One thing about Wolfe Toners, they have a passion for soccer. You can always expect a hard game from Wolfe Tone.

The match we played against them in the Vevay was a real cracker. We played top form, Wolfe Tone the same. There was a right crowd at the game You could sense it was something special. We even had butterflies in our stomachs going out on the pitch. The crowd was roaring, cheering Wolfe Tone on.

Liam Molloy, our manager, felt like he was leading out Man Utd against Man City. He had left his grubby coal-crusted jacket and trousers at home and given himself a good scrubbing. He looked nice and shiny. Even his clothes looked nice and shiny.

Jesse Ryan, the Wolfe Tone manager, kept pacing up and down the sideline, shouting his head off. He was supposed to be urging his players on, but he got that carried away he began to call us names. We'd curse back at him, and that only made him madder, until, finally, the ref had to call us all together and put an end to it. Only we didn't; we kept it up out of earshot.

We had a nickname for Jesse Ryan. We called him Jesse James. You'd be sure of a good chase if you called him that.

The two teams dug into one another – all very fair – fair but tough. Two minutes to go we scored a real sickener. From a corner, two yards off the goal-line, the ball struck our Redser Byrne on the private parts and spun into Wolfe Tone's net. Redser collapsed in agony. As for us, we were over the moon. Delighted, we carried him to the sideline and left him with Liam Molloy to recover.

Two minutes later the match was all over.

We had won 0-1. Redser still felt sore going back down the town. He'd gone a bit bandy. But it was worth it. Anything was worth it to beat Wolfe Tone.

'You beat us, but you won't win the street-league,' mouthed Jesse Ryan when we were leaving the pitch. 'You won't win the street-league!' he repeated.

'Neither will you, Jesse James,' we shouted, and ran for dear life.

And they wouldn't win.

Good old Redser Byrne!

5 Flintstone and Mad Victor

I never thought it would be so hard to write a book. I mean, having to sit there, trying to think. Putting up with my da moaning all the time, Ma in and out, and my sisters getting in the way.

Sometimes I wish my sisters were good-looking and had lots of boyfriends. That way they'd never be in the house, doing their hair, painting their faces, all that kind of carry-on. They get on my nerves. The only time they're in demand is at Hallowe'en.

Still, I thought, I'll struggle on with the book. Write, write, write, as long as the words keep coming.

The baldy lad, the man who was talking on the telly about writing, was on again last night. He was talking about 'flow'. The words flow out like a river, only you don't get wet. The pages get wet with words. Brill, isn't it?

What was more, the baldy lad said

something else that really interested me. Some crowd in Dublin were running a competition for the best story written in the 14–16 age bracket. I really liked that. He gave an address to send entries to. I wrote it down.

If I got my story finished in time I'd enter, maybe win the competition, and be famous. There would be a prize for the winner; a computer and a hundred pounds spending money. Well, he said 'A hundred pounds'. I added the spending money bit, because I'd spend it for sure. I'd have to before Da would get his hands on it.

I'd already got my book off to a good start. I was going to be in it, but I decided not to. I'd keep myself for the sequel. I'd call myself Shane, after the old cowboy picture Alan Ladd was in. Why? Because I look like Alan Ladd, that's why.

But getting back to the book: I mention going through the estate where I live. 'Going through the estate's congested intestines,' is how I put it. Don't ask me how I thought it up, but I did. I was just after looking at a leaflet

Ma picked up at the doctor's. There was a coloured drawing of a person's insides. The image took root and I put in in the story.

Another image was of the time I went out to Howth with a few pals. It was rainy and drizzly – that got in the story too, the rain and the drizzle. I had the lads walking past the waste ground on our estate, where the cider-drinkers meet. I had them going to football training.

It was all paying off for me now. It was getting me into the start of my story. There was a bullet in the breach, so to speak. All I had to do was pull the trigger.

If I got the time, that is.

Another uproar. The Da nearly put his head through the telly. He tripped over the cat. It was the nearest he'll ever come to being on the nine o'clock news.

We beat the lard out of Charnwood in the street-league. They were mostly rugby players who went to Pres, Bray. They were more used to handling a ball than kicking it.

'They should 'ave all played in goal,' said 'Flintstone' McKay, our outside-left.

'There's rules, ye know. Only one can play in goal.'

'I know that.'

But Flintstone didn't really know. Rules meant nothing to him. He didn't know how to play in a position either, although he also played for Riverside Boys. He'd go all over the pitch, chase after the ball wherever it went. If he could have flown, he'd have gone up in the air after it.

But we did manage to pound one rule into

his thick skull. It was the only rule he understood. Well, it wasn't a rule of the game. It was a special rule we had made up for him:

'Never go into our penalty area.'

We were that afraid he'd give away a penalty.

Flintstone is a bit dim, but he's very fit. Nobody on two legs is as fit as him, not even an ostrich. Some day he's going to win the Olympics. He was born to run, just like that fellow in the film, *Forrest Gump*. Only Forrest Gump wasn't for real; Flintstone is.

During training we'd do lots of laps. Flintstone always kept running after we'd stop. A few times we'd be going home after training and Flintstone would still be running around the pitch.

'What are you doin' that for?'

'Nobody told me to stop.'

'Well, you can stop now.'

That's the way with Flintstone McKay. You have to tell him everything. He's more than a bit dim.

Some of the others on our street-league team

also play for Riverside Boys. They're all nuts, but 'Mad' Victor is the nuttiest. Not only is he mad, but he looks it. He's always staring at people, especially people he doesn't like.

He hates referees most. He's always cursing and arguing with them. The only referee he likes is Harry Hennessy. Harry used to ref all our home matches, but he's retired now. He helps out with one of the teams.

Mad Victor really loves Harry Hennessy. Harry is big and fat, and lots of fellows slag him. But not Mad Victor. He's real nice to him.

'Why are you so nice to Harry, Victor?'

'Cause he's me da.'

'He's not your da.'

Mad Victor didn't have a da. Luckily he was born without one.

Of us all, Mad Victor loves football most. He'd play night and day. He's better playing street football, because there are no refs, no nothing, just a free-for-all. Playing in the street-league and with Riverside Boys he gets sent off every now and again.

Once Victor is anywhere near the ball he's

just left to get on with it. He'll play any position, even goal-keeper.

'Like playin' in nets, Victor?'

'Yeah.'

'Why?'

'Cause it makes me feel like I'm Tarzan.'

Just after we played Charnwood, that night, we were going down the Main Street. Mrs O'Leary's picture was hanging from all the street poles.

'What's she doin' on the poles?'

'Can't ye read?'

'Course I can. What's she in, the circus?'

'No, the elections. She's standin' for the local Council elections.'

'What Council?'

'The one that meets in the Town Hall. They talk about the town – that kind of thing.'

'Gossip, ye mean?'

'Naw, plan how they're goin' to improve things. An' instead they go out an' make a mess.'

'Mrs O'Leary wants to be one of them?'

'Yeah, cause she'll be able to go to the meetin' an' bawl them all out, like she does her oul' lad.'

'Think she'll get voted in?'

'Course she will. Between all the relatives she has and all the relatives *they* have, she's bound to get loads of votes.'

'Know wha'?' spouted Mad Victor.

'Wha'?'

'Tha's why she started this street-league.'

'Why?'

'To make herself known, so as to get votes.'

And maybe that *was* why Mrs O'Leary had started the street-league. We all thought she was doing us a big favour. But, like Mad Victor said, the only big favour she was doing was probably for herself.

Mad Victor wasn't all mad. Sometimes he talked sense. He was only one hundred per cent mad when he played football.

6 The Rhode Island Red

Chippy was beginning to talk about his gran again, her being a banshee and that. He told me she'd been down at Fitzgerald's farm the last few weeks – on holidays.

'Is that so?'

'Yeah. I found one of Mad Victor's football boots in Midge Baker's garden. He must have thrown it at Midge's rotweiller and the dog brought it home. It was lying in Midge's front garden beside a rose-bush. I recognised the boot straight away. There's a big slit in it, only

it's much bigger now.'

'What's that got to do with your granny?'

'I was bringin' the boot back to Victor. His house is beside the graveyard. Me gran was sittin' on the wall, with a Dunnes Stores bag.'

'What was in the bag? Guinness?'

'No, hen eggs. She likes raw eggs for her breakfast ... You don't believe me, do you?'

'No.'

'She likes hens as well. So do I. She used to keep them when she lived in the house at Purcell Square. Ever see the house in Purcell Square, Jimmy?'

I didn't bother answering. Why should I? What he was going on about was too much for anyone to believe. Even Mad Victor would hardly believe what Chippy was coming out with. Even though I heard the banshee howl that night in the graveyard I didn't believe a word he was saying now.

'I never really saw the house in Purcell Square where Gran an' Granda lived. All I remember was boarded-up windows, weeds hangin' from the chimney and window-sills, damp all up along the outside. When I was eight it collapsed in a heap. They put a hoardin' up around it and left it for months before takin' it away by the lorry-load. It's a gap now in a row of houses. It's like when you open your mouth and smile and there's a tooth missin' in front. That's what it looks like – bloody awful.

'They can't do anythin' with the site. Gran and Granda never left a will, so nobody knows who owns the place. Me ma an' da don't want to know for starters, cause they haven't got the money to do anythin' with it anyway.

'How could they? We only live in a council house. Gran an' Granda had money, but they spent it all before they died. They would have sold the house too, only when they died it took them by surprise.'

Chippy asked me to go to the graveyard with him. He wanted to show me something. As it was the middle of the day I didn't mind. I had nothing else to do anyway.

'Climb over the wall.'

'Why, Chippy?'

'Cause the gate's locked an' what I want to show you is in the graveyard. An' keep quiet, very quiet.' Chippy took me straight to his granny's grave. There was a hen roosting on the headstone.

'What d'ye think of that, Jimmy? It's a Rhode Island Red.'

'Where did you get it?'

'Me granny took it from Fitzgerald's farm. It's great for layin' eggs.'

'The caretaker'll run it out of the graveyard.'

'Him! He's too lazy to do anythin'. See the length of the grass, all the weeds: He'll do nothin', much less catch Daisy.'

'Daisy? Is that what you call the hen?'

'Yeah, Daisy Buttercup.'

'Daisy's a cow's name, Chippy.'

'Not to me. Daisy's the sun, the moon, an' the stars. There's goin' to be more hens too. I'll have loads of eggs an' I'll sell them around the houses. People go mad for fresh eggs. I'll have at least three dozen eggs a week by the time I'm finished.'

'I thought you said the eggs were for your granny?'

'They are. I'll sell the leftovers.'

'It's your hen, isn't it, Chippy?'

'What d'you mean?'

'You took it from Fitzgerald's farm, didn't you?'

'No, it's Gran's.'

'Give off!'

'Honest.'

Honest? Chippy didn't know the meaning of the word.

Just then I did something stupid. I told Chippy about the book I was writing.

'Wha' kind of book is it, Jimmy?'

'Football.'

'Tell me a bit about it.'

So I told him.

Soon as I told him he seemed to lose interest and changed the subject. He went on about all the hens he'd have in the graveyard over the next few weeks. He couldn't stop talking about that, and all the money he'd make from selling the eggs. There'd be no problem, he said.

'The only problem'll be the caretaker. But me gran will take care of him. She'll give him a good banshee scarin'. He'll be afraid to go near the hens in case she'll put a curse on him. Me gran'll fix him proper. He believes in banshees ye know. Gran gave out a banshee call the other day an' he ran for his life. It was real cool. Want to come up to Fitzgerald's farm an' we'll get a few more hens?'

I could just imagine the Ma's face if I was caught nicking hens, so I said, 'No, I'm not a tea-leaf. Let's go down the Park an' have a kick-about instead.'

So we went down to the Park and played football for a while. Pretty soon we forgot all about hen eggs, banshees, all that kind of stuff. The 'Hungry Hill Banshee' could go to Fitzgerald's farm and nick the hens herself.

'Hungry Hill Banshee'? That was what Chippy was calling his granny now. He was even getting some fifty-pence pieces from some of the smaller kids on the estate. He'd send them down to the graveyard but they'd never see anything. Once or twice they'd hear a howl and that would be it.

But the Hungry Hill Banshee was beginning to make a name for herself. Sometimes late at night she could be heard howling. People on the estate were beginning to talk about her.

Soon as that happened the Hungry Hill Banshee was on the road to fame.

7 A Battered Husband

Most of us who played for Riverside and for Palermo in the street-league went to school. That's except for Mad Victor. It wasn't so much that he didn't want to go; he just wasn't allowed in. We envied him. But he envied us. He found it boring, walking around all day with no one to talk to.

Apart from us, the lads who played football, everyone else gave him a wide berth. They were all afraid of him. He was something like the Hunchback of Notre Dame, only he didn't have a hunched back or a bell to swing from.

All the lads who played for Riverside felt sorry for Mad Victor. After school he'd always be waiting for us outside the school gate. He'd run over and start hugging us, he'd be so delighted. If he had been a dog he'd have wagged his tail.

I always went to school with Chippy O'Brien. Like I've probably said, he's from

Fassaroe, a great footballer, and plays with us for Riverside Boys. But in the street-league he'd be against us, playing for Fassaroe, Mrs O'Leary's favourite team.

Chippy brought up the idea of me writing a book again. He was a little unusual for a fellow who was into football. He had an artistic streak.

'When you write,' he told me, 'you have to write about stuff you've suffered over. That way you'll really care an' only write the best.'

'Who told you that?'

'No one. I just know. You have to know about the pain.'

'That's why I'm writing a football story. I know all about pain. An' I've suffered too, standin' in the rain, waitin' to come on as a sub, bein' cursed for makin' a mistake, squelchin' about in muck. I suffered all right. I did more than me bit.'

The next time Mad Victor and I were coming out of Fassaroe we passed Mrs O'Leary's house. She was in the garden with her sleeves rolled up, hanging out the washing.

Mad Victor called her an oul' bags to her face.

'Jim, come out here!'

Jim was Mrs O'Leary's husband.

Fassaroe was different to most estates; it housed a battered husband. Within two seconds flat we were looking him straight in the eye. At least Mad Victor was. As for me I was already half way down the road.

'Give it to him, Jim!'

But Jim didn't react. It was evening-time

and he'd had enough conflict for the day.

'Are you goin' to stick up for me, Jim O'Leary? Don't let them call me names. Be a man. Stand up for your wife.'

But Jim couldn't stand up for himself, much less his wife.

Just ask Mrs O'Leary. Just look at the dents on her handbag, her frying-pan, and everything else she battered her husband with.

Mad Victor gave her one last insult and took off down the road after me.

'If you win the street-league you won't get much, I'll see to it. You pup, you jail-bird, you fatherless hooligan.'

Either way, if we won the street-league we wouldn't be expecting much, not from Mrs O'Leary anyway.

Two days later we played Oldcourt away. Oldcourt were managed by a Scotch lad. 'Aberdeen Eddie' we called him. He was mad keen on the street-league. But it was being played at a bad time for him as some of his players were down to play Gaelic football most nights the street-league games were on. Luckily they were off playing Gaelic when we played Old-court. The match ended in a draw.

Aberdeen Eddie was very disappointed with the result. He knew if he had had a full team he would have beaten us. So did we. He was a good loser though. He shook our hands. Nobody ever shook our hands before, so we kind of felt sorry for him. He even gave us a few cans of Coke. We told him if he was ever stuck for a few players we'd play for him now and again – that is if the other team didn't know we were Palermo players. But he said he'd be okay, he'd make do the way he was.

Some of the teams in the street-league were like that; always stuck for players, like the two Woodbrook teams and Seacrest. A lot of their players were eleven and twelve-year-olds, some only nine. One estate had a player who was nineteen. But he only looked twelve. Nobody ever complained about him. He was hopeless anyway.

'One of God's children,' Harry Hennessy said.

'He don't look like a saint to us, Harry.'

'That's not what it means.'

'Wha' does it mean then?'

'Nothin' much. Just somethin' you turn a blind eye to.'

We let it go at that.

Ardmore, too, had a problem with players. Once summer came they were always coming and going on holidays. Us, we never went on holidays, except maybe a day's outing with the Summer School Project. But most of us were barred from that.

Anyway it was good to get an away draw against Oldcourt. Whatever about the other teams, we knew we'd have to beat Fassaroe, Wolfe Tone and Oldcourt at home to keep in the running to win the street-league.

We were really hard set on winning Mrs. O'Leary's crummy league so as to spite her, just to throw the lot back in her face when we won. It meant that much to us. Everything! Well, almost everything – my book excepted.

On our way home from Oldcourt, down the town and across the bridge to Palermo, Mrs

O'Leary's picture was still tied to every pole. It was getting close to the local elections, and already she was doing the rounds of all the estates, knocking on doors and all that.

She was standing as an 'Independent' – whatever that was.

'"Independent" is a person who stands for election on their own. They don't belong to any political party. They do everythin' on their own.'

'You sure?'

'Course I'm sure. They're independent of everybody else, like they do everythin' themselves an' don't want any help.'

'Mrs O'Leary's no Independent then. She had all her kids and grandkids givin' out leaflets. You should see the leaflets, they're on copybook pages. And you should see the spelling. Mad Victor'd do better.'

None of us who played for Palermo in the street-league wanted to see her win. We pulled down some of her posters. Others we filled in with black eyes and beards, and changed her name from Brenda O'Leary to Brendan

O'Leary of the Battered Husbands' Party.

We even did a bit of legwork for her, usually about eleven o'clock at night, shouting through letter-boxes, 'Vote for Mrs O'Leary, you oul' bags.'

We did our bit. If Mrs O'Leary got elected it wouldn't be our fault. We tried really hard. We couldn't do any more than that.

8 SOB's Ear

Chippy came banging on my door the other day. He asked how I was getting on with my story – what had I written so far – that kind of thing. I told him. I also told him about the competition that was mentioned on the telly, that I was going to enter my book (it was a bit more than a story now, more a book). He got even more interested when he heard about the competition. He wanted to know where to send the entries.

When I told him he seemed to smile for a second and went on to moan about his granny giving him a hard time the night before. He said he had to go down to the graveyard and tell her to stop howling like a banshee. He insisted on giving me a blow-by-blow. Dead boring.

'"Gran, what's wrong?"

"It's your grandad's anniversary.'

"What d'ya mean?"

"It's the anniversary of his death."

"Gran, could you keep the howling a bit low? Maybe we could go somewhere where you wouldn't be heard."

"Like where?"

"Maybe go to where Mrs O'Leary lives."

"Where's that?"

"Fassaroe."'

Could you believe it? Chippy was a barefaced liar. Saying he went up to Fassaroe with his gran to make sure she got as near to Mrs

O'Leary's house as possible, so as to give her a real good banshee scaring. He said Mrs O'Leary tried to make her husband get up out of bed and put an end to the ghostly racket.

'It's the banshee, Brenda.'

'It's a cat. Get up and run it down the road.'

'I won't!'

'Do as I say!'

Next thing, there was a family row. So Chippy said. Jim O'Leary got battered again. But he wouldn't go out.

Chippy's granny didn't get back to the graveyard until half-four in the morning.

Daisy Buttercup was waiting for her on top of the headstone. She'd just laid an egg. Gran stroked Daisy Buttercup. Sucked the yoke from the egg, wiped the last tear from her eye and went asleep for the day.

Her husband's anniversary was over for another year.

I took one look at Chippy. 'How'd ye come up with a story like that? It's you should be writin' a book, not me!'

'I don't wanna write a book, not yet anyway

... You don't believe me about my gran bein' a banshee, do you?

'No.'

'You heard her howl, didn't you?'

'That could have been anythin'.' Maybe even you.'

'Half of Bray believes in her now. They can hear her all over the place.'

'Someone told me Mad Victor gave you one-fifty to see her.'

'I gave it back. He wanted to bring a catapult. I wouldn't have him usin' a catapult on Gran. Someday soon somethin' will happen an' you'll really believe me gran's a banshee ... Know what? Had a great idea for your book. It'd walk that competition you told me about, no bother.'

'What's the idea?'

'I'll tell you again – I've to be up the town for three. An' don't forget, me gran'll scare the wits out of you some night. You'll know for sure she's real then.'

I stood outside the hall door and watched Chippy go down the road. He had some nerve. I wondered what his great idea was. Maybe, if I wrote a second book, I'd use the idea; that's if he told me. Whatever it was, it would be sure to be a pack of lies.

Still, the best of books were lies.

Like mine.

Only some told the truth.

The street-league was passing quickly. We were winning all our remaining matches. There were only two games left. Our second last game was at home to Wolfe Tone in the People's Park. It would be down to the winners and Fassaroe to decide who would win the competition. Our last match would be against Fassaroe, also at home.

Most of my friends, both in the street-league and playing for Riverside, like to call other fellows names. Like if you had a big head we'd call you 'Big Head', a big nose, 'Snozzle' or 'Snottser' – things like that.

There was this lad with big ears who played for Wolfe Tone. They stood out a lot. If you used your imagination you could let on they were wings, they stood out that much. We weren't the only ones who called him names. Lots of the fellows called him names like 'Batman', 'World Cup Ears', 'Floppy Ears', 'Ear-Lingus'.

He took it all to heart. His mother brought him to the doctor, and the doctor took pity on him. He said, 'We can do something with those ears, take a slice off the back and pin them.'

The lad was sent to Temple Street Hospital and a doctor operated on his ears. When he had finished the lad had ordinary ears, the same kind of ears as everyone else. Nobody would be able to call him names any more. After the operation the doctor put a bandage around the lad's head. Told him not to take it off until he came back in four weeks' time for a check-up. 'Give the ears time to heal.'

When we played Wolfe Tone in the Park the lad was there, his head bandaged and his football gear beside him. His name was Stephen O'Brien, only his mates called him SOB. He was a pretty good player. They were thinking of playing him. But on account of his operation they were afraid to, and said they'd only put him on if things went badly.

Things did go badly. They were losing 1-0, so they put him on, only the ref told him to take the bandage off his head. That was the first time we saw him with ordinary ears. They looked great. And we all knew he was real proud of them.

A few minutes to go, and still a goal down, Wolfe Tone got a throw-in near our endline. SOB went over to take it, because he had a long throw and could reach our box, no bother. But in his rush to take the throw his ear brushed off Harry Hennessy's linesman's flag.

We nearly all died on the spot. SOB's ear fell off. Most of us saw it fall and lying on the ground. We all got a good look at it.

Harry Hennessy picked it up, yelled for a bottle of milk, put the ear into it, bandaged SOB's head and had him rushed to Temple Street.

We saw SOB a few weeks later. His head was still bandaged. We saw him some time

later and his ears were all right. You could pull at them, anything, and they'd never fall off.

As for the match, we won

That left us at home to Fassaroe in our last match. The street-league was between us and Fassaroe. Between us and Mrs O'Leary. That was the way we looked at it. We wanted to beat them real bad.

'So bad,' said Mad Victor, 'that even their own mothers wouldn't know them.'

Not that bad, but bad in a footballing sense.

9 *Forlorn Love*

I came up with a brilliant idea for the book yesterday. I told Chippy O'Brien about it on the way for a swim at the seafront.

'Me da left a tax form on the table yesterday mornin'. I filled it in for him and sent it off. I didn't bother tellin' him. He's been lookin' for it everywhere, even in the breadbin. If the tax crowd come lookin' for him, they'll send him to jail.'

'You don't like your da. Why?'

'I just don't like him, that's all. Want to hear how I filled in the tax form?'

'How?'

'I put big block capitals on it: DESEASED. SEE YOU IN HELL. If that doesn't cause trouble nothin' will. Great idea though.'

'Put it in the book.'

'I would, but I'd be afraid Da would cop on to what happened the tax form.'

'He'd belt ye?'

I didn't bother answering Chippy. But there was no way Da would belt me. He'd be too lazy, that's why.

About then, matters really came to a head between us and Mrs O'Leary. She was going up the town one morning to do her shopping when she came across Mad Victor climbing up a pole to pull down one of her posters.

Victor was about half way up the pole, just out of reach of getting a belt of Mrs O'Leary's handbag.

That didn't stop him from getting a tongue-lashing, though. But he was quick enough to give it back before sliding down the pole in double-quick time and darting down the street as fast as he could.

'I know who you are,' Mrs O'Leary shouted after him, the veins in her neck bulging with rage. She always swelled up when she got mad – swelled up like a frog and went red in the face – gloss-paint red.

We knew Mrs O'Leary would be at the match between us and Fassaroe in the Park.

We knew she'd be there to spot Mad Victor, on account of having caught him climbing the pole after her poster. We were in two minds whether to play him or not. But we put him out on the pitch anyway. Not to annoy Mrs O'Leary or anything like that. But because he was one of us, one of the team.

We would be loyal to him.

I'm going to have the two sisters in the book after all. I'm going to have them living on an estate, just like the one I live on. I might even have my da in it as well. I'm going to make him blind though. He'll have a guide-dog and the guide-dog will lead him everywhere.

I'm keener than ever on writing my book. I'm getting ideas from everywhere. I just have to get up in the morning and I've loads of ideas. I get them in the middle of the day, too, even at Mass. I jot them all down and save them up for later.

If I write the book, and it does really well, I'm going to buy a Suzuki and go and live in the country, Indian-style. I have this thing about Indians, I like them a lot. And I'll have a squaw. And I'll wear war-paint.

It'll be a lot better than the school uniform we wear. It's grey and black, although we all don't wear the full rigout – some have the grey, others the black. We're kind of rebels. It's a rule among the kids that nobody wears the full uniform. It's a tradition we have. Wear the full uniform and you'd never get to see the school gate.

After I wrote the first two chapters of my book I had a change of heart. Like I've said, the story started out as a football story, but after the first two chapters I began to change everything. But first, I want to tell you how I got to the end of the second chapter.

Ma had cleared out the box-room and turned it into a kind of study so that I could get on with my book in peace. Nobody was allowed into the room once I was there. I had a sign outside on the door: DO NOT DISTURB.

Chippy gave it to me. He had a part-time job as a bell-boy in a local hotel. He took it off one of the doors and gave it to me. It wasn't just a Joe Soap black-and-white sign. It had a touch of class to it. Even in our house it meant that whoever was behind the door was someone important. It looked the part.

Although the sign, and Ma, kept everyone out of the room while I was writing, I could hear the noise of the kids playing outside and the cars going by. But the sound coming through the window helped me. If there had been total silence I don't think I would have been able to write. I wasn't used to absolute quietness. I had only been in the real country about twice in my life.

I was used to sounds in the house, and the noise of kids and cars on the road, and maybe the din of a row, or a sing-song from some of the crowd going home from the pub.

But the rows and sing-songs were in the middle of the night. Luckily I don't do my writing late at night – unless I get a sudden surge of inspiration. But by the time I find the pen and jotter it has long gone cold – as cold as my bare feet on the lino.

The reason I had a change of heart about my football story was that Chippy came around to the house and asked to see me. We went upstairs to my room.

'That book you're writin'... that football story...'

'What about it, Chippy?'

'You're still writin' it for that competition on telly, aren't ye?'

'Yeah, it has to be in by the end of the summer.'

'I think you're only wastin' your time writin' a football story for a competition, especially if you want to win.'

'What d'you mean?'

'Football stories never win competitions... Here, give us a look.'

I passed him over my two chapters.

He read it. Shook his head. 'How does it end?'

I told him what I was trying to write, trying to make it sound exciting.

He shook his head again. 'The judges wouldn't even look at that. They'd throw it straight in the dust-bin.'

'Do you think so?'

'Course I do. You wouldn't stand a chance.'

Maybe Chippy was right. Probably was, because all the judges would no doubt be oul' lads and oul' wans who had never played football in their lives and hated anyone that did. And they'd hate a book about kids playing football even more. Because in their minds kids playing football would all be rowdies, like what would go around banging on their doors at night, and giving them cheek.

No, maybe Chippy was right. My football story wouldn't stand a chance. Still, I felt bad about giving up on my idea. Imagine, no Harry Hennessy, no Mr Glynn, no Riverside, no Chippy, no Mad Victor. Nothing about the street-league, nothing about Mrs O'Leary. And I was hoping it would be the greatest football story ever written. But maybe I could write it some other time. Maybe in the future.

'But I want to write somethin', and football is all I know.'

'Gotta great idea for a story,' said Chippy. 'It's all about years ago. About this pipe-band havin' trouble with the law. They're marchin' up an' down the town playin' rebel songs, an' the police tell them to stop playin' rebel songs, cause the police belong to Britain, an' the story is set in the eighteen-somethin's an' we were under the British then.

'So the police don't want the band to play those rebel songs, but the band won't stop an' they go up Bray Main Street, an' there's a riot.

An' the priest an' all get involved. An' some of them get arrested an' sent to jail. An' they won't let the band play in Bray any more. So they get the train to other places an' cause trouble there.'

'Sounds mad.'

'It ain't. It's great. Let me tell you more: There's this quare lad, he's the band-leader, an' he's causin' all the trouble. He falls in love with this wan who follows the band, only he gets arrested an' sent to jail, only they won't let him out, not until they put him on a ship an' send him to Australia. When the one finds out he's bein' sent to Australia, she goes crazy an' goes to war against the law, she becomes a Fenian, or somethin'.'

'Nobody'd believe any of that.'

'So what, it's only a story.'

'They'd only rubbish it. They'd say it's stupid. That a story like that could never happen.'

'Well, it did happen. An' the one that went crazy an' became a Fenian, she was my gran's granny.'

'An' the lad that was sent to Australia, was he her husband?'

'No, she met him afterwards.'

'I just couldn't write a story like that. I'd be laughed at.'

'No, you won't. They'll all look up to you. An' I've a great title for it: *Forlorn Love.*'

I knew only too well nobody would look up to me. None of the lads I went to school with, or played football with, liked books. They were only interested in what I was writing because they thought it was a football story and I had said most of them would be in it.

But if *Forlorn Love* turned out the way Chippy was talking about it, what with stodgy oul' bagpipers and drummers knocking the lard out of the police, and one of them getting sent to Australia with Chippy's gran's granny crying on the quayside, I'd be the laughing stock of the town.

My only hope was to stop writing straight away. But Chippy would have none of it. He said it was a great story and deserved to be written. He said if I didn't write it he'd leave Riverside Boys and join Wolfe Tone.

I didn't want that to happen. Chippy was our best player. Mr Glynn and Harry Hennessy wouldn't like it. Neither would the team. I'd have them all on my back if Chippy left. I'd have to take the blame, and I didn't want that. So I decided to have a go at writing the story.

Forlorn Love: a soppy love story.

Bloody hell!

10 The Fassaroe Final

Lately Chippy was in the habit of coming to my house and sneaking up the stairs to see how I was getting on with the new story.

After I got all about the pipe-band causing trouble down on paper, he came up with a few extra ideas for the band-leader, the fella that was sent to Australia. He had a name for him too – Felix Healy.

'Chippy, nobody'd believe I'd write a story like that. An' the soppy love scenes are kinda embarrassin'.'

'Well, it all happened. An' it's yours. Your name'll be on the cover. *Forlorn Love* by Jimmy Quinn. Sounds kinda cool, doesn't it?'

'No, Chippy, it's daft. They'll think I'm gone off me rocker.'

Chippy tried to convince me that *Forlorn Love* would be better than any football story.

'It'll have more appeal, more vigour,' he said, whatever he meant by that. 'And think of the angles! Social problems. Young love – that'll get the oul' wans. The poor gettin' trod into the ground. Torture in the jails.'

He was a pretty good talker. After three or four visits to the house, he began to win me over. I actually began to feel real keen when he told me what was going to happen later in the story: Felix Healy mining for gold; Felix Healy fighting the British Crown; Felix Healy rescuing thirty kangaroos from a bush-fire.

And all the time Chippy's gran's granny, alias Kathleen Devine, was back in Ireland pining away, her one true love far away in Australia, praying for the day he'd come back.

The more he talked, the more my imagination got carried away. I forgot all about Kathleen Devine. Instead I let on she was Heather McFadden, a girl I knew from school. Heather McFadden was older than me and the best-looking girl in our school. As soon as she heard I was writing a book she began to act real friendly. She wanted to know if I'd go to the pictures with her. She had to do the answering for me. I completely froze.

Two days after the pictures I did something real daft. I asked her around to the house to see if she could do something for my sisters' appearance. I don't know why I did it. I suppose it was sheer fright. But I did it anyway.

'Can you do somethin' for my sisters?... For their looks?... They're kinda plain lookin'?'

'Yes, sure,' she smiled.

That smile really got to me. It still does. It was like climbing up a mountain, and finding there, on the far side, was everything you ever wanted. Know what I mean?

Well, Heather McFadden came around to the house with loads of cosmetics She had them in a fancy-looking hold-all. Ma said it was like the Avon lady, whoever she was.

I had planned to watch what was going on but they made me leave the room. But I saw a bit through the keyhole.

By the time Heather had finished there was a total transformation. When they came downstairs my sisters looked definite eight-and-threequarters. They couldn't wait to go discoing.

The match against Fassaroe finally happened. Whoever won would be the street-league champions. Us against Fassaroe, at home in the Park. At least we'd have decent sized goal-posts. Nothing would favour Freddy Fox. Not unless he prayed that hard he'd be granted a miracle and grow two feet overnight.

Mrs O'Leary was there too. She had a kind of suitcase with her as well as the one she always carried. We more or less knew what would be in the suitcase – the trophies for the street-league. She surprised us when she said there'd be a trip to Butlin's for the winners.

A trip to Butlin's! And there'd be something

for the runners-up. Maybe a set of shoddy medals if she thought it would be us. She hadn't forgotten Mad Victor scurrying up the pole like a squirrel to pull down her election poster. What was more, he was given the number 9 jersey. But that didn't mean anything. He'd be all over the pitch, chasing after the ball, his sweat flowing in rivers like hot steam, and a glaze in his eyes as if the guards were after him.

Mr Glynn and Harry Hennessy had come along to watch the game. They took a neutral stance, as they had players on both sides. Having some of our club-mates playing for Fassaroe didn't matter to us, or them. All we wanted was to win the match. Not just to defy Mrs O'Leary but to be on the bus for Butlin's and enjoy the day out. We were all really set on the idea of going to Butlin's.

'Butlin's, where's that?'

'Mosney.'

'Where's that?'

'Somewhere down the country.'

'I always thought Butlin's was in England?'

'Naw, there's one in Mosney as well.'

'It's not a Mickey Mouse one, it is?'

'Naw, it's good. Mad Victor was there last year. Said it's great. The train stops right outside the place.'

'Why are we goin' by bus, then?'

'Cause Mrs O'Leary doesn't want us on no train. Says it'll be easier to keep an eye on us, in case we cause trouble.'

'What does she think we are? Tea-leaves?'

'Yeah, of course she does.'

And we were, Fassaroe and us. We were both the same. That's why we all played for Riverside Boys. We had a kind of feeling for Riverside. We belonged. The shoes fitted.

Quite a crowd had gathered. Most of the adults from the two estates had come down to the Park to watch. All our parents, all our uncles, all our aunts, that kind of thing. Even the really young kids, anyone who could walk.

With the local election only two days away it was a great chance for Mrs O'Leary to show herself off to everyone. She got the main trophy out and placed it on the flat of the suitcase, in around the half-way line, where everybody could see it.

It was a big cup, almost as big as the FA Cup. We all had a good look at it: The Brenda O'Leary Perpetual Cup.

'Wha's "perpetual" mean?'

'Somethin' to do with Hell, I think.'

'Naw, it means every year, from year to year. It'll be played for every year.'

'Does tha' mean we'll have to come back again next year?'

'Naw. It says U-14. We'll be too old. It'll be for the lads younger than us.'

'No it won't. If we win an' I like Butlin's I'll be back again next year. I'll play in me little brother's name.'

So would we all. That's if we had little brothers. We'd all be back. But I wouldn't. I didn't have a little brother.

As a point of interest, Mad Victor had a little brother. His name? 'Mad' Henry. He was at the match and all. He had this funny cap on him. It looked kind of Chinese, only it wasn't. It was a lampshade. He found it on top of a

dust-bin on his way to the Park. He liked it, so he put it on his head and let on it was magic, that it made him invisible.

He spent the duration of the match going around calling everybody names. That was until he came to Mrs O'Leary. She swung around and gave him a thump of her handbag. She knocked the magic lampshade off his head and broke it. He knew he wasn't invisible any more and went into a fit of tears.

Mad Victor had to come off the pitch to console him. They had to get someone to play in his place, it took such a long time. Then he wanted to sort out Mrs O'Leary for hitting his brother, but one of the big lads grabbed him and took him behind the goal-post until he cooled off.

It didn't end up too good for us on the pitch either. We got beaten 0-1. Chippy O'Brien did the damage again. He scored off a corner. The ball was knocked out to him. He met it on the volley and sent the ball straight into the top corner of the net.

When the final whistle went Mrs O'Leary was only beaming. She was delighted to see us get beaten. Double-delighted when she saw Mad Victor and his brother totally in the dumps.

She presented Fassaroe with the tickets for the trip to Butlin's and handed us shoddy 'silver' medals she must have taken out of the bottom of the dust-bin Mad Henry got his magic lampshade from. They were horrible, dull, silver things, with a lop-sided harp on them. They didn't look like football medals at all. They looked more like what you'd get for Irish dancing. We felt proper fools.

Mr Glynn and Harry Hennessy came over to try and cheer us up. It was just as well. Liam Molloy, our manager for the street-league, didn't want to know. He picked up our football gear, put it into the kit-bag and went off without saying a word. We hardly ever saw him again, except sometimes coming from work, the coal dust cemented to his clothes.

He'd been thinking of becoming a football manager, of one day taking Old Trafford by storm. But now it was all over, the dream was no more. His street-league team had got beaten, the team he'd togged out in Man Utd colours, the team he'd filled the jerseys with, and numbers and all – Ryan Giggs, Roy Keane, Eric Cantona and all that. We'd got beaten and in Liam Molloy's eyes we weren't Man Utd anymore. We were just us, with our crummy runners-up medals and a few flattened fags for after the match.

Later we found out that the ref. was a brother of Mrs O'Leary's who lived down the country. He'd come up to Bray for the weekend and she asked him to ref. Probably told him to rob us. Some of his decisions were crap, especially the one that led to the goal.

If we had known who he was we would have kicked up. But we didn't know until it was too late. Not until he was gone down the country again. But we wouldn't forget him in a hurry.

Thinking back, he was the spitting image of Mrs O'Leary. He looked like her to a tee, except for the dress, long coat and handbag.

It wasn't our fault we got beaten. We tried our hardest. We wouldn't have won anyway. Not even if we were Pele, George Best and Paul McGrath rolled into one. Not with Mrs O'Leary around we wouldn't have won. Like her old trophy, she was top of the heap. And would be. Perpetually.

From that moment on we really hated her.

11 Mrs O'Leary's 'Do'

A few days after the match with Fassaroe, Chippy asked me to go to the graveyard with him. There was a big brown rooster perched on his granny's headstone and, directly behind it, Daisy Buttercup was crouched on the ground, her feathers all spread out like an umbrella.

'Chippy, what's the rooster doin' here?'

'That's Daisy Buttercup's new husband. He came down from Fitzgerald's farm to court her, an' he won't go back.'

'What's up with Daisy Buttercup, with her feathers all puffed out?'

'She's sittin' on eggs. She's goin' to hatch them out.'

'You mean she's goin' to have chicks?'

'Yeah, her an' Horace Bluebell.'

'Who's Horace Bluebell?'

'Her husband, the rooster.'

I'd heard it all now. The chicks would

probably have daft names as well. I rememb-ered Chippy saying he was crazy about hens and poultry, but I didn't think he'd be as bad as this. A few months' time and he'd probably have the graveyard full of hens.

'If the chicks hatch out, how're you goin' to feed them, Chippy?'

'I'll feed them all right. I'll go up the town an' buy some Chick Crumb.'

I didn't know much about hens, but seeing Horace Bluebell was a cock, he was more than likely to start crowing real early in the morn-ing. I sized him up. He was right big, with a fat throat – there'd be plenty of crowing from him. He'd definitely have the half of Hungry Hill up bright and early in the morning. He'd cause havoc all right. The place was set to turn into a regular mental dump.

I knew we wouldn't get out of the grave-yard without Chippy mentioning his granny and the banshee bit. He saved it up until last.

'There's a lot of people talkin' about Gran. They're seein' her all over the place.'

'Is that so?'

'They've seen her in her black shawl an' long skirt. She scared the livin' daylights out of them.'

'You don't say?'

'Yeah, I do say. But she won't let you see her cause you won't give me any money towards buyin' her Guinness.'

'Well, I'm not handin' over good money for nothin.'

'It's not for nothin'. You'd see a banshee. Not everybody sees a banshee.'

'Who's seen her then?'

'Flintstone McKay seen her.'

'Then I don't need to see her, not now.'

'What d'ye mean?'

'I'll just ask Flintstone what she looks like.'

'You will?'

'I will.' And I did.

Flintstone said she looked real scarey. And she howled a lot too. But he didn't think much of her howl.

'What do ye mean?'

'It was more like a croak.'

'Did you run for it?'

'No, I didn't. I just left, kind of slow like.'

Slow? Flintstone didn't know the meaning of the word.

Flintstone ran. He always ran.

Even with all the talk, and Flintstone saying he saw the banshee, I didn't really believe it was true. I had a sneaky suspicion there was something up, and that Chippy was behind it.

I even went to the graveyard a few times during the day and there were no empty Guinness cans in the place.

If there was a banshee, there should have been empty Guinness cans. And no Guinness cans meant no granny, no banshee.

Well, that was how I saw it. And I didn't believe I was far wrong. How could I when I'd never seen a dot?

Mrs O'Leary got elected to the town Council. She held a 'do' in one of the local hotels. All her family and relatives were there. They filled the place up. There was just barely room to fit all of them in. Me and Chippy O'Brien saw some of them going in. A few of her sisters came over from England; they looked just like her. She had her husband in tow, but he was afraid to speak to anyone. He just sat there, and ate and drank whatever was put in front of him.

How did we know?

Mad Victor's uncle was a waiter in the hotel and we found out from him.

They had a band at the 'do' and all the young O'Learys, dozens of them, got up to dance, but Mrs O'Leary wouldn't let them. She made her husband sing a song instead: *I'll take you home again, Kathleen.* The song made Mrs O'Leary all mushy and weepy Some of her sisters began to cry, the ones with the Birmingham and Manchester accents.

The night turned into a song contest after that, nothing but old-fashioned songs, one after the other. All of them got up and sang. All except the younger ones. They bolted downstairs to the disco.

So Mad Victor's uncle told us.

They had a great time. Mrs O'Leary couldn't walk home. They had to carry her.

We really liked that bit – Mrs O'Leary being carried home. It made our day.

By the time Mrs O'Leary got elected, most of the book was falling into place. Felix was out in the bush, half parched with thirst. There were vultures and wild budgies flying around the sky, just waiting for him to die.

I thought the bit about the wild budgies was out of place so I went to Chippy to ask him were there wild budgies in Australia.

'Chippy, budgies would hardly be flyin' around waitin' for Felix Healy to die?'

'They were. That's how it was told to me.'

'Did he die?'

'No, he was rescued by aborigines.'

'I bet he became their leader, Chippy?'

'No, soon as he got better he left them.'

'What then, Chippy?'

'He prospected for gold.'

'Bet he got gold, too?'

'Plenty. An' he sent back to Ireland for Kathleen Devine to come an' join him.'

'Did she go?'

'No, she'd become a rebel an' was on the run. Felix's message never reached her.'

'An' they never met after that, Chippy?'

'No. In the end she married my great-grandad an' everythin' that happened between her an' Felix Healy was at an end.'

'Pity, it would've been better if she caught a fever an' died.'

'What'd make it better?'

'It'd be sadder, a better endin' for the book. It'd make her out to be like Molly Malone. She died of a fever, an' they wrote a song about her. Maybe they'd write a song about Kathleen Devine if we had her dyin' of fever in the book. Why not, Chippy?'

'Naw, it'll have to be as it was. There'll be no changes. You leave the story as it is.'

There was another matter on my mind. My love affair had turned sour.

Heather McFadden! I couldn't get her out of my mind. Her name sent shivers through my spine. She used to love me once, so she told me. It's hard to believe she ever loved me She wouldn't look at me now.

The only thing I can think of is that my da must have annoyed her. Maybe the time she came round to fix up the sisters he appeared in a dirty old shirt, and slippers with his toes sticking out.

I don't know. It must have been something. It was all my da's fault. Everything is my da's fault.

I liked blaming Da. It makes me feel good. Once I wrote a poem about him:

Da,
    Why
        When you
            Go down the garden,
There's nothing
            In the tin can?

Da,
    Why
        When you
            Go to the supermarket,
There's nothing
            In your pocket?

Da,
    Why
        Is there
            Always nothing?
Nothing on the table?
            Nothing in your life?

Maybe it wasn't much of a poem. But that was my da: *The Nothing Man.*

12 Mad Victor's War-dance

Even though I no longer meant anything to Heather McFadden, I decided to dedicate the book to her. Maybe when she saw her name in print, she'd change her mind about me. Everything was fine until Chippy objected.

'Chippy, I'm dedicatin' the book to Heather McFadden.'

'Heather McFadden from school?'

'Yeah. She's mad keen on me, Chippy. She's always pesterin' me about the book. Says she's inspirin' me to write it.'

That wasn't strictly true of course, but I could hardly tell him the real truth, could I?

'Inspirin' ye, is she?'

'Yeah. That's why she wants me to dedicate it to her.'

'It's my ideas that are goin' into the book. Mine an' my gran's. So never mind Heather McFadden. Dedicate the book to my gran's memory or else...'

'Or else what?'

'She'll go around to your house an' haunt you.'

'Haunt me?'

'Yes!'

And Chippy's granny *did* haunt me. One night I was in the house on my own. I was upstairs in the box-room thinking about Heather McFadden. I could hear noises outside. The dogs were all barking.

Next thing I heard a scratching noise on the window. I went over to the window to see what the noise was. I nearly died of fright. There was this ugly face looking in at me.

About the same time, unknown to me, Mad Victor was coming down the road. He was finishing off a bag of chips. He squeezed the empty bag into a ball and gave it a kick. He watched it go up in the air. And that's when he saw the banshee on the drain-pipe, next to the box-room window.

Soon as Mad Victor saw her she began to wail. Hall doors opened and people came out to have a look. Only Mad Victor didn't want to see any more; he took off down the road.

Soon as I saw the banshee's face in the window I got to hell out of the room. I ran downstairs and hid. I didn't come out from where I was hiding until Ma, Da and my two sisters came home.

I told them about the banshee.

Ma didn't believe me. Nor did my sisters.

Da did though. He was into ghosts, banshees, the lot. He believes in everything – everything except Santa Claus and Cinderella. He got straight on the phone and rang Father Bourke, our parish priest.

The next day Father Bourke came around to the house. He said prayers and doused the house in Holy Water. Gallons of it.

While he was in the house, Ma told me that when Father Bourke was baptising me he nearly drowned me. She said he had this thing about water. Maybe he shouldn't have been a priest but should have joined the Fire Brigade instead.

What we didn't know, not until one of the neighbours saw Father Bourke coming out of

the house and told him, was that the banshee had been spotted climbing down the drainpipe. Bill Hanley, from two doors down, chased her up the road, and caught up with her in Midge Baker's front garden. He grabbed the banshee by her black shawl and pulled the ugly plastic mask off her face.

And who was it?

Only Chippy O'Brien, the 'Hungry Hill Banshee'.

With Chippy found out, I was off the granny

hook. So I was keener than ever to dedicate the book to Heather McFadden. But she wasn't too keen once I gave her a sneak look at what I'd written so far.

Then I had a change of heart.

I decided, after all, to dedicate the book to Chippy's granny.

That is: Brigid O'Brien, R.I.P.

Daisy Buttercup, Horace Bluebell and the little ones were causing big trouble down at the graveyard. Chippy couldn't control them and they were all over the place. Although the graveyard was big, a lot of it was covered over with concrete and marble chippings. There wasn't enough for them to eat. They were getting over the graveyard wall and going into people's gardens and helping themselves to what was on offer. All the time Daisy Buttercup's family was getting fatter, and in no time at all people hadn't much left in their gardens.

I had a word with Chippy about it.

'I know,' he said. 'Some of the oul' wans are eyein' them up these last few weeks. Only problem is catchin' them. I know the hens'll end up in a pot pretty soon, worse luck.'

'They wouldn't put'm in a pot, would they?'

'Course they would. They all love roast chicken around here. Oul' Midge Baker'd love a few in her oven. I could have done with bein' the Hungry Hill Banshee a little longer, cause that helped keep the hens safe. Nobody'd interfere once they thought she was for real. They'll probably even nick the eggs now, let alone the hens.

'I definitely coulda done with bein' the Hungry Hill Banshee another bit – even if only for the rest of the summer. The kids were beginnin' to give me good money to see her too. An' the eggs were sellin' a bomb. Don't know where I'll get a few bob now. Gettin' caught that night outside your house has cost me a fortune. I was savin' up to buy a new pair of football boots. I was goin' to buy a Liverpool kit. I was even goin' to buy Ma a woolly jumper. Now I can forget about the lot.

'Those hens are gettin' right and big. Any week now they'll be ready for the chopper.

Like I said, they're bein' well eyed as it is. What d'ye think we should do?'

'Simple. We'll move them back to Fitzgerald's farm. They'll be safe there.'

Chippy agreed.

He wanted to move the hens straight away. I told him to wait until later in the night, wait until they were roosting, that way it would be easier to catch them. Not just that, but I didn't want anyone seeing me chasing around a graveyard after hens. Anyway, I wanted to go off and get some cardboard boxes to put the hens in, and that would take time. It was all right for Chippy. He thought everything could be done at once.

No, it would take time to round up Daisy Buttercup and company. And it would have to be done properly, not having them running loose, squawking all over the graveyard.

We went back later that night. The hens were all droopy-eyed. We caught them, no bother, put them in boxes and brought them up to Fitzgerald's farm.

I didn't get home until 1.30 a.m.

'Where were you?' asked my da.

'Movin' house for someone,' I replied, and went upstairs to bed. I was knackered.

And that's how the hens got back to Fitzgerald's farm. We knew they'd be safer there.

So too did Daisy Buttercup, Horace Bluebell and all the little ones.

Chippy O'Brien told us all about Fassaroe's trip to Butlin's. They left on the Friday and didn't come back until Monday afternoon. They loaded all their baggage under the flap at the back of the bus. Not that they had much luggage, but they loaded it carefully anyway.

Mrs O'Leary went with them. She wanted to oversee things. Make sure that everything was done properly. That they'd all behave and not turn the trip into a total disaster.

She stood at the door of the bus as they got on. She had a big box of lollipops and sweets which she handed out.

The Fassaroe lads sneered at the lollipops. They were more into cigarettes and the likes. But Mrs. O'Leary thought she was doing them a favour and it made her happy.

For days before the trip Mad Victor pestered Chippy O'Brien about going to Butlin's. On account of being there before, it was the one place in the whole world he really wanted to go to, except wherever it was in America that the cowboys and Indians hung out. He was dead keen on cowboys and Indians, especially Billy the Kid, Jesse James and Geronimo.

Chippy agreed to smuggle him on the bus. While Mrs O'Leary was handing out the lollipops, Chippy was helping Mad Victor to hide under the flap among all the Man Utd, Celtic and Liverpool football bags.

'Don't forget to let me out when we get to Butlin's,' he croaked, his eyes peeking out from beneath the pile of bags.

'I won't.'

True to his word, Chippy let Mad Victor out soon as they got to Butlin's. He kept him out of Mrs O'Leary's sight all weekend, well almost.

On the last night they had a party in one of the chalets. The party wasn't official by reason

that it wasn't Mrs O'Leary's idea. The Fassaroe lads thought it up among themselves, and it soon got out of hand.

There was a lot of shouting and acting the fool. Mad Victor was stripped to his underpants with war-paint streaked all over him, and a few feathers he'd pulled from a turkey that was part of the Pet's Corner in Butlin's. He was letting on he was an Indian, whooping and hollering, and doing a war-dance on top of one of the beds in the chalet.

Suddenly, someone shouted, 'Mrs O'Leary's comin',' and they went all quiet. Mad Victor made a dive and hid beneath a bed. Only his ankle was sticking out, and almost as soon as Mrs O'Leary walked into the chalet she saw the ankle and yanked it out.

Out slid Mad Victor, underpants and all.

Mrs O'Leary got an awful fright. She screech-ed and ran out through the door. She didn't realise it was Mad Victor. Just thought it was some savage.

The lads grabbed Mad Victor and bundled him out the back. They brought him down to the boat-house, where there's a lake – boats go out on it during the day. They hid him there and told him not to come out until it was time to go back home to Bray.

'But I'm freezin'.'

'We'll get your clothes.'

'I'm starvin'.'

'There'll be some grub in the bins, we'll get you that.'

'Don't forget to get me back on the bus.'

'We won't.'

'Make sure. Cause I'd never be able to get to Bray if you don't. I wouldn't know where I was. An' cannibals might get me.'

'There's no cannibals here. Ye've to go to Africa to get cannibals.'

'Is Africa near here?'

'Course it's not. It's thousands of miles away.'

'I'll be safe then?'

'Sure you'll be safe.'

And Mad Victor was safe, once he got over the night in the boat-house and Mrs O'Leary had calmed down. Chippy smuggled him on to the bus – no bother.

The first Mrs O'Leary saw of him was when they got back to Fassaroe. She saw him run by the bus and off down the road.

'Is that Mad Victor?' she asked.

'Yeah.'

'What's he doin' runnin'?'

'Trainin' for the Olympics.'

'Thank God we didn't have the likes of him with us in Butlin's.'

Thank God, indeed.

13 Disaster!

I finished writing the book a few days ago. I felt great seeing it all lying there, and flicking through page after page of words. Thousands of them. And when I lifted all the copybooks together the weight made me feel humble; all those words, all those pages.

All that had to be done now was to get it typed. Brains O'Mahony, a fellow from sixth year in school, had a sister who was a typist. She typed so fast, you couldn't see her fingers move – so Brains said.

So I brought all the copybooks to Brains' sister. She said she'd start typing it out at once. She wasn't going to charge me either. She said it would be an honour to do it for nothing.

I could hardly wait to see *Forlorn Love* typed and looking neat and tidy. Two weeks' time and it would be ready for the competition – and it *had* to win. A few months later it would be a book – I hoped. Then, I'd be on the telly, and all that. And *Forlorn Love* would be on the bookshelves. A best-seller!

I have plans to write another book. The story I had intended to write in the first place; my own story all about Riverside. Mad Victor will be in it – and Chippy. It will be the greatest football story ever written.

But something went wrong when Brains' sister was typing out the pages I had sweated over. Her house got broken into and *Forlorn Love* went missing. We found some pages later scattered on the roadway and in a few front gardens. The pages were soggy and splashed in mud. It was impossible to make out the words. So that was the end of *Forlorn Love*.

'I should've had another copy of the book,' I told the lads.

'You sure should have.'

'You don't believe me?' I said to the lads. 'That I wrote a book?'

'No.'

And they didn't believe me. They thought the pages I was showing them could have been some office papers that had blown off the back of a dustbin lorry.

But I'd pick myself up and start all over again. I could picture the lads, saying, 'Aren't you comin' to football trainin'?'

'No, I'm goin' to write a story.'

'Another so-called story!'

'Yeah, another story.'

'See you.'

'Yeah, see you.'

There was one page not marked, one half page, with two heart-breaking words right at the bottom.

I kept it as a souvenir. And what were the last two words written on the page?

Guess.

Still don't know? Well, I'll tell you:

'The End.'

And so it was the end.

So long.

Farewell.

Goodbye.

The End